AIDS

AIDS

EXAMINING
THE
CRISIS

TOM FLYNN   KAREN LOUND

LERNER PUBLICATIONS COMPANY
MINNEAPOLIS, MINNESOTA

The authors would like to thank Conrad J. Storad, director of research publications, Arizona State University, and Lorraine Teel for their assistance with this project.

Copyright © 1995 by Tom Flynn and Karen Lound

Library of Congress Cataloging-in-Publication Data

Flynn, Tom, 1946
    AIDS : examining the crisis / by Tom Flynn and Karen Lound
    p.   cm.
    Includes index.
    ISBN 0-8225-2625-5
    1. AIDS (Disease)—Juvenile literature. 2. AIDS (Disease)—Social
aspects—Juvenile literature. [1. AIDS (Disease) 2. Diseases.]
I. Lound, Karen. II. Title.
RA644.A25F59 1994
362.1'969792—dc20   94-13326
                                                               CIP
                                                                AC

Manufactured in the United States of America

1 2 3 4 5 6 I/SP 00 99 98 97 96 95

Contents

INTRODUCTION

As this book goes to print, millions of people in the United States and around the world have been affected by an illness called AIDS—*a*cquired *i*mmuno*d*eficiency *s*yndrome. AIDS is caused by a virus, a microscopic organism that can grow and multiply inside living cells. The AIDS virus is called HIV, or *h*uman *i*mmunodeficiency *v*irus.

HIV attacks and disables the body's immune system— the system that normally fights off illnesses. When the immune system breaks down, a person with AIDS will develop life-threatening illnesses.

Hundreds of thousands of people are dead as a result of AIDS. Millions more are infected with the virus that causes AIDS. For every person actually infected with HIV, however, there are dozens more—family, friends, lovers, children, caregivers, and even casual acquaintances— who are also affected by AIDS. It is likely that you too will be touched by AIDS sometime during your lifetime.

The day will probably come when you know someone who has AIDS. When that day comes, we hope you'll react with sensitivity and understanding. Encouraging

Joey DiPaolo, who contracted HIV through a blood transfusion, speaks about AIDS prevention to other high school students.

sensitivity about AIDS is one goal of this book. The most important goal, though, is to give you the information you need to avoid contact with HIV, the virus that causes AIDS.

AIDS first appeared in the United States in the early 1980s. Many people contracted HIV before anyone even knew the virus existed—let alone how to prevent infection. The AIDS outbreak was so rapid and widespread that scientists called it an epidemic.

We now know that HIV is transmitted, or passed from one person to another, through the exchange of blood, semen, and vaginal secretions. The activities that are most likely to transmit HIV are sex and the sharing of hypo-dermic needles during drug use.

Many people who have been infected with HIV are men who engaged in homosexual behavior. That is, they had sex with other men. AIDS first appeared in the United States in the gay (homosexual) community. Other people, however, contracted the virus through hetero-sexual activity (sex between a man and woman), inject-ing drug use, or blood transfusions.

In this book, you'll learn how HIV is transmitted, how AIDS affects the body, and the medical treatments avail-able for people with AIDS. You'll also learn how society has responded to the disease, particularly in the areas of politics, education, and public health. You'll read about the controversies and myths surrounding AIDS, as well as the future of the AIDS epidemic.

Most importantly, you'll learn how to protect yourself from AIDS. You'll learn about safer sex—ways to reduce your risk of HIV transmission during sexual activity. You can avoid infection, but you need the right infor-mation to do so.

Scott Miller is one person who didn't have the right information. "I didn't get any education about AIDS until I was a senior in high school," he says in the Summer 1993 issue of *10 Percent* magazine, "and by then it was too late. . . . I figure I was infected before I even had a chance to learn about safe sex." Scott tested positive for HIV infection at age 18, in 1986, and was diagnosed with AIDS at age 23.

We now know that specific behaviors put a person at risk for becoming infected with HIV. These behav-iors include sex and drug use, and they are discussed, in detail, in this book. Talking about AIDS isn't always easy. "AIDS is about sex, drugs, and rock and roll—and death," says AIDS educator Lorraine Teel. These subjects make many people uncomfortable. Teaching people to avoid HIV infection isn't easy, either. Because sex is private, natural, and common to our lives, many people are slow to change sexual behaviors that carry a high risk of HIV infection. People often don't make smart choices when they are using drugs. All of these obstacles stand in the way of AIDS prevention.

Because gay men and drug users were the first people in the United States to get AIDS, many people think that if they aren't gay and aren't shooting drugs, then they're safe from infection. That's not true. Anyone can get AIDS. But you can avoid contact with HIV and AIDS if you have the right information. We'll give you that information in this book.

1
A Modern Plague

In early 1981, young, otherwise healthy gay men in places like New York, Los Angeles, and San Francisco were showing up in doctors' offices with strange illnesses. Some of the men had *Pneumocystis carinii* pneumonia (PCP), an infection of the lungs. Others had Kaposi's sarcoma (KS), a type of cancer that usually strikes elderly men of Mediterranean descent. Still others had thrush, a cakey, white yeast infection in the mouth and throat. By late August 1981, more than 100 cases of PCP and KS had been reported in the United States. Forty percent of the patients had died.

Doctors reported these strange cases to the Centers for Disease Control (CDC) in Atlanta, Georgia—the federal agency in charge of monitoring and preventing the spread of disease. The CDC is considered the world's foremost "medical detective agency."

Researchers at the CDC were concerned and began studying what some feared was the start of an epidemic. They discovered that all the patients had something in common: immune deficiency. Their immune systems, the network of cells that normally fight off illnesses, could not fight anymore. The researchers had to figure out what was making the men sick.

First they gave the new sickness a name. Because the initial cases occurred in gay men, some health professionals named the disease GRID, or *gay-related immunodeficiency*. These professionals knew that epidemics don't usually strike people based on their sexual lifestyle, but the only thing these first patients seemed to have in common was that they were men who had sex with other men.

A few reporters picked up the story, and soon people were reading and hearing about this new "gay disease." Since most Americans believed that the disease struck only gay men, they thought they were safe from infection.

By 1982 hundreds of people, still mostly gay men in big cities—Los Angeles, San Francisco, and New York—were sick and dying. While doctors and researchers couldn't find a cure for acquired immunodeficiency syndrome, or AIDS, as the disease was now called, many were coming to the conclusion that it was caused by a virus. They also determined that the virus was being spread through the exchange of certain body fluids—mostly during sex or through shared drug needles.

Research on the AIDS virus was led in the United States by Robert Gallo of the National Cancer Institute and in France by Luc Montagnier of the Pasteur Institute. Gallo called the virus HTLV (human T-lymphotropic virus), and Montagnier called it LAV (lymphadenopathy-associated virus). An international committee gave the virus its official name—human immunodeficiency virus, HIV—in 1986.

A virus is a microscopic organism that can attack cells and cause disease. Viruses do not attack just certain groups of people. They can find their way into any living body. In 1982 new groups began getting AIDS: people who had injected drugs (heroin, for instance), prostitutes, and women who had sex with bisexual men (men who have sex with both men and women).

Researchers had a lot more work to do, but they needed money to do it, and they needed it fast. By mid-1982, the death rate for people who had been diagnosed with AIDS for two years was up to 75 percent. (What researchers didn't realize was that a person could be infected with HIV for many years—10 or maybe more—before becoming sick. By the time these early AIDS cases were diagnosed, many patients were already in the late stages of the disease.) Officials at the Centers for Disease Control knew they had an epidemic on their hands. They tried to alert the medical establishment—doctors, public health officials, and researchers—about the crisis. They also tried to convince the federal government, including President Ronald Reagan, to fund research on AIDS.

Meanwhile, gay men began to form groups to care for people who were suffering with and dying from AIDS. One of these groups was the Gay Men's Health Crisis in New York, and another was the San Francisco AIDS Foundation—both formed in cities hard-hit by AIDS. These groups tried to convince the government to provide money for research on HIV and for special centers to care for people with AIDS.

But in the first year of the AIDS epidemic, the federal government gave the CDC only $1 million to study the outbreak—compared with $9 million spent to research

Legionnaire's disease, an illness that killed 29 people in 1976. One million dollars wasn't enough. By May 1982, the AIDS epidemic had spread to 20 states and had killed 136 people.

Neither the government nor the media seemed to be paying much attention to the epidemic. During the Tylenol painkiller scare in 1982, when seven people died from cyanide-laced capsules, the *New York Times* ran a story on the incident every day for the entire month of October and 23 more in November and December. During that same October, 260 Americans died from AIDS. But in the last three months of 1982, only 15 stories on AIDS appeared in all the nation's leading magazines and newspapers combined.

Why were so few people paying attention to this killer disease? To many, the answer was obvious. AIDS was striking mostly gay men, and many Americans did not approve of homosexuality. Some people believed that AIDS was God's punishment for homosexual behavior. Dr. James Fletcher wrote in a *Southern Medical Journal* editorial that homosexual men were reaping "expected consequences of sexual promiscuity."

"The poor homosexuals," wrote newspaper columnist Patrick Buchanan, "they have declared war upon nature, and now nature is exacting an awful retribution."

People made similar comments during the bubonic plague, or Black Death, of the Middle Ages. They said that plague victims had brought the disease upon themselves. In later centuries, cholera and leprosy victims heard the same thing. The first people to get these diseases were often poor and lived outside of the society's mainstream. Most AIDS sufferers, now including gay men, drug users, and prostitutes, were also outside of the mainstream. California Congressman Henry Waxman explained the situation this way:

> There is no doubt in my mind that if the same disease had appeared among Americans of Norwegian descent, or among tennis players, rather than among gay males, the response of both the government and the medical community would have been different.

At the end of 1983, AIDS began to appear in a new group: people who had received blood transfusions. Some had received transfusions during surgery. Others had tranfusions as part of their regular treatment for a blood defect known as hemophilia. Researchers realized that the AIDS virus was being spread through the nation's stored blood supply.

In March 1984, the CDC counted 73 blood-transfusion AIDS cases. Of these 22 had died. In 1985, when a test was made available, blood banks started testing all donated blood in the United States for HIV.

With the discovery of HIV-infected blood, some Americans became more sympathetic to AIDS sufferers. But others still believed that "bad people" were causing the epidemic. Some even suggested that HIV-infected people were deliberately donating blood and contaminating the nation's blood supply.

About the same time AIDS was discovered in people who had had blood transfusions, it was found in another group: babies. Most were infected by their mothers' blood, either while still in the womb or at the time of birth. Stories about HIV-infected babies appeared in newspapers and on radio and television. More people began to pay attention to the epidemic.

Then, in 1985, Rock Hudson—movie star, sex symbol, and good friend of Nancy and Ronald Reagan—announced that he had AIDS. Throughout his long career, Hudson was a popular heartthrob and adored by many female fans. Most people assumed he was heterosexual. But the newspapers revealed that Hudson had contracted AIDS from having sex with other men. His fans were loyal, however, and the American public did not abandon him because he had AIDS.

Journalist Randy Shilts writes that after Hudson's announcement, "the epidemic had finally hit home."

Movie star Rock Hudson, pictured here in the 1960s, was the first famous person to reveal that he had AIDS.

Because Rock Hudson revealed that he was dying of AIDS, the American people finally faced the disease, four years after it had killed 5,000 Americans.

Also in 1985, researchers devised a test that would tell people whether or not they had HIV. Although commonly known as the AIDS test, the test actually detects the presence of HIV in a person's blood. People infected with HIV are said to be "HIV positive," and they are almost certain to develop AIDS. The HIV test was an important milestone in the fight against AIDS. Unfortunately, the test also paved the way for discrimination against people who were HIV positive.

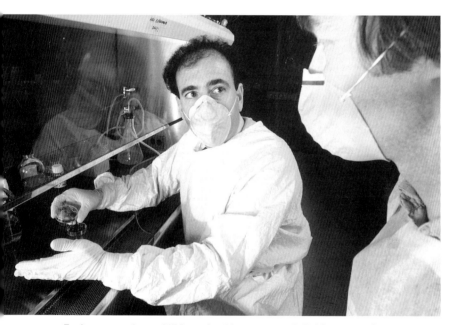

Early research on HIV at the University of California in San Francisco.

As the 1980s came to a close, the government was beginning to offer more support in the fight against AIDS. In May 1987, President Reagan announced that he would appoint an 11-member commission to advise him on the epidemic. Also in May, the President delivered his first speech about AIDS to the nation. By that time, 36,058 Americans had been diagnosed with the disease, and 20,840 had died.

AIDS was not just an American problem, though. The disease had appeared in Central Africa many years before it was known to Western scientists. In Africa HIV spread mostly among heterosexual people and often went unreported. Travelers who contracted HIV through sex or drug use carried the virus to other countries throughout the world. When it reached big cities in the United States, infection rates soared.

When the first AIDS sufferers were infected (many years before they were diagnosed with AIDS), nobody knew about HIV. Nobody knew that having sex or injecting drugs increased a person's risk for getting the virus. Today we know what behavior can expose a person to HIV, and we know how to prevent the spread of the virus.

Doctors don't yet know how to cure AIDS. Most doctors believe it is always fatal. Medical researchers are working hard to discover a cure or maybe a vaccine, a preparation that would increase the body's immunity— or resistance—to HIV and prevent infection. In the next chapter we'll learn more about the AIDS virus. We'll also find out how doctors treat AIDS and learn about the quest for a vaccine and a cure.

2
A DEADLY VIRUS

A virus is a microscopic organism. Once a virus enters a living cell, it can reproduce itself hundreds or even thousands of times. It can infect cells, damage them, and cause disease. Normally, when a virus or another disease-causing agent enters your body, your immune system responds—fighting off the infection and helping you get well.

Most viruses reproduce in a specific part of the body. Viruses that cause colds, for instance, infect the respiratory system. The human immunodeficiency virus, the virus that causes AIDS, reproduces in the immune system itself—attacking the system and making it incapable of fighting off disease.

HIV and the Immune System

White blood cells known as T-helper cells play an important role in the immune system. Their job is to quickly alert the rest of the immune system about an infection. Once these cells have sounded the "red alert," other cells go to work to fight the infection. Without the T-helper cells, the immune system can't send out

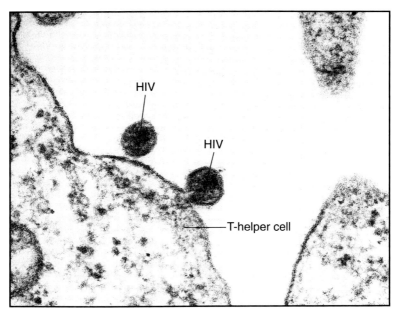

HIV

HIV

T-helper cell

The human immunodeficiency virus (HIV) as viewed through a microscope. The virus appears as two dark circles attached to a T-helper cell.

fighter cells. The infection remains in a person's body and causes sickness.

The average healthy person has around 1,200 T-helper cells per cubic millimeter of blood, although some people have a lot more and some people have fewer. Generally, the fewer T-helper cells a person has, the more likely he or she will get sick with an infection.

HIV does its damage by attacking T-helper cells. The virus penetrates the cell, changing its genetic material (the part of the cell that is preprogrammed to sound the red alert for the immune system). Not only does HIV disable the T-helper cell, it also turns the T-helper into a

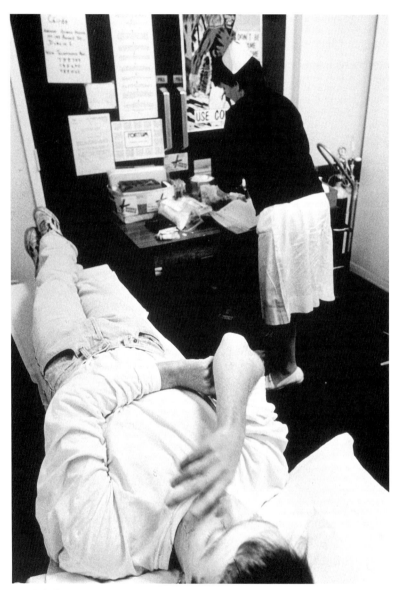

An AIDS patient receives medical treatment at a clinic in Ireland.

cell that can produce more HIV. As the process continues, there are fewer and fewer T-helper cells to tell the rest of the immune system that an infection has entered the body.

The destruction of T-helper cells occurs over the course of many years after a person has been infected with HIV. In fact, a person might be infected with HIV for 10 years or more and still not get AIDS. But as the T-helper cells are destroyed, the immune system grows weaker, and the risk of infection increases. Often, the person will develop one of many illnesses associated with AIDS.

The average person usually becomes vulnerable to these illnesses sometime after the total T-helper cell count drops below 500 cells per cubic millimeter of blood (although it is possible to have a very low T-helper count—50, for example—and still not have an AIDS illness). As a person's T-helper-cell count drops, doctors often prescribe medications to help bolster, or strengthen, the immune system.

Eventually, when a person does not have enough T-helper cells left to fight off specific infections, a doctor will give the person an AIDS diagnosis. (Babies with HIV often develop AIDS sooner than adults, because their immune systems are not yet fully developed.)

Up until January 1993, health professionals gave HIV-infected people an AIDS diagnosis only if they had an AIDS illness, as labeled by the Centers for Disease Control. In early 1993, however, the CDC expanded its definition of AIDS. In the new approach, in addition to people with AIDS illnesses, anyone with a T-helper cell count of 200 or less is also said to have AIDS.

AIDS Illnesses

Researchers have identified 26 illnesses associated with AIDS. Some of these illnesses are called opportunistic infections (OIs), because HIV weakens the immune system, giving other viruses and diseases an opportunity to infect the body.

Opportunistic infections can occur at any stage of HIV infection. But the illnesses are particularly severe in the later stages of AIDS, when the patient's immune system has been greatly weakened, and he or she can no longer fight off infections. Some common OIs are:

- *Pneumocystis carinii* pneumonia (PCP), a type of pneumonia, a lung disease
- *Mycobacterium avium* complex (MAC), caused by bacteria. The infection commonly lodges in the intestines or stomach, although it can infect other parts of the body.
- cytomegalovirus (CMV), a virus that generally lodges in the intestines or stomach. CMV is a common but usually harmless virus, until it is recruited by HIV. Then it attacks areas such as the liver, the central nervous system, and the urinary tract. It may also cause retinitis, which is blurry vision leading to blindness.
- lymphoma and Kaposi's sarcoma (KS), forms of cancer
- cancers and infections of the reproductive system in women

Other illnesses commonly associated with AIDS are wasting syndrome and AIDS-related dementia. Wasting syndrome involves rapid weight loss over a short period of time. AIDS-related dementia involves a deterioration of the mind, similar to Alzheimer's disease. It is characterized by confusion, forgetfulness, and a loss of basic mind functions.

Doctors care for HIV-positive and AIDS patients with a variety of treatments. They prescribe antibiotics and antiviral drugs to fight opportunistic infections. Patients with cancer receive radiation and chemotherapy treatments. Many patients take azidothymidine, or AZT. This drug is able to slow the destruction of T-helper cells in some HIV-infected people.

When a person with AIDS requires extensive or round-the-clock medical care, he or she might be hospitalized

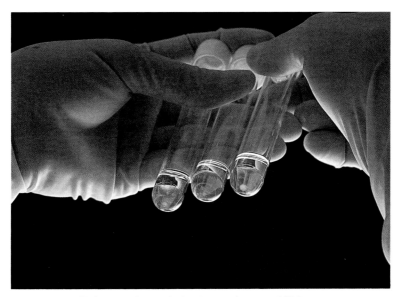

The drug AZT has prolonged the lives of some AIDS patients.

or moved to a nursing home. Despite new drugs and treatments, opportunistic infections weaken and usually kill people with AIDS. But both patients and doctors agree that medical treatment buys time—it keeps the patient alive longer, sometimes for many years.

Before his death in 1994, Grant Gates talked about how it felt to live with AIDS. "I take each day of health as a wonderful gift," Gates said, "and each illness, infection, or hospitalization as part of my life. Slowly, I know, my body will not bounce back."

The Fight in the Laboratory

Once inside the body, viruses are hard to fight—because drugs that can damage viruses can also damage healthy cells. Instead of treating viral infections with drugs, doctors often try to *prevent* viral infections by using vaccines. A vaccine is a weakened or killed version of a virus that is introduced into a person's body. Even though the vaccine virus is harmless, the body still recognizes it as an intruder and fights it off. If the real virus later enters the body, the person's immune system will have developed defenses to defeat it.

We now have vaccines for many viral diseases, including smallpox, polio, and measles. Our successes with vaccines led to optimism in 1983, when researchers discovered that AIDS too was caused by a virus. Prominent scientists, including Jonas Salk, the man who developed the vaccine for polio, joined the hunt for an HIV vaccine. Some researchers predicted that doctors would develop a vaccine for HIV within 10 years.

More than 10 years later, we still don't have a vaccine. Why not? There are a number of reasons. One is that HIV has turned out to be far more complicated and mysterious than other viruses. HIV can multiply in glands called the lymph nodes for years before it begins to attack T-helper cells. Researchers still don't know how or why the virus decides to emerge and begin its killing spree.

HIV is also capable of changing its basic structure, creating new strains, or variations, of itself while within a person's body. This fact causes extra problems for researchers. If they were to develop a vaccine based on the known strains of HIV, the vaccine would work on only those strains, not any new ones that might be developing in the bodies of HIV-infected people.

Scientists agree that finding a vaccine for HIV will take a long time—time for testing and careful, thorough research. Many researchers now doubt that we'll have an effective HIV vaccine before the year 2000. In the meantime, scientists are hoping to find a treatment that might turn AIDS into a condition that is chronic, or ongoing, but less often fatal. Similar treatments have been discovered before. For instance, diabetes was once almost always fatal. Now, with the help of a hormone called insulin, many diabetics live as long as do people with normal health.

Until researchers find a vaccine, a cure, or a life-prolonging treatment, people with HIV and AIDS are also finding ways to help themselves. Many people have responded to their HIV or AIDS diagnosis by making changes in their lives to improve their health. Some of these changes are improving nutrition, exercising, getting off drugs, and reducing stress. Doctors believe that these efforts may make AIDS patients less susceptible to infections and prolong their lives.

3
HIV: TRANSMISSION AND PREVENTION

L et's talk about what HIV is not. HIV is not a germ floating in the air. It cannot be transmitted by casual contact such as kissing, touching, or sharing forks and knives. HIV is, in fact, a fragile virus that is very difficult to transmit. To infect you, HIV must enter your bloodstream.

Once in a person's bloodstream, HIV will eventually find its way into other body fluids. But only the exchange of blood, semen, vaginal secretions, or breast milk will allow HIV to pass from one person to another. Body fluids such as tears and saliva cannot hold enough of the virus to permit transmission. To prevent infection with HIV, avoid behaviors that will put you in contact with the blood, semen, or vaginal secretions of a person who might have HIV. One such behavior is sex.

Transmission through Sex

Many young people are sexually active. If you think you are ready for a sexual relationship, you should be aware of the risks related to sex and be able to talk about these risks with your partner. These risks include unwanted

A volunteer in New York City hands out condoms and information about AIDS prevention.

pregnancy and sexually transmitted diseases such as gonorrhea and herpes. Another risk is contracting HIV. With the right education, you can avoid these risks.

It takes knowledge, skill, and maturity to talk with your partner about HIV. Has your partner been tested for the virus? Has he or she had many previous sexual partners? Has your partner ever injected drugs?

Remember that people often carry HIV for many years before getting AIDS. People with HIV don't usually look sick, and many do not know they are infected. Only the HIV test can determine whether or not someone has the virus.

Talk to your sexual partner about HIV. If he or she isn't willing to talk openly about past sexual relationships or drug use, perhaps you shouldn't have sex with this person. If you do choose to have sex—no matter who your partner is—make sure you help protect yourself from HIV by using a condom.

When a man and a woman have sex, he may place his penis in her vagina. This behavior, known as vaginal intercourse, involves semen and vaginal fluid. Blood might also be present if, for example, a man has a sore on his penis or a woman is menstruating. If any one of these fluids—blood, semen, or vaginal secretions—contain HIV, the virus could pass from one partner to the other. Tiny tears, or pinpoint breaks, in the skin of either the penis or the vagina could give HIV a point of entry into the bloodstream.

A man may also put his penis into his partner's rectum. This practice is called anal intercourse, and a man may have it with a woman or with another man. Pinpoint breaks in the lining of the rectum also give HIV ready access to the bloodstream.

Transmission is most likely to occur during sex when a man ejaculates HIV-infected semen or pre-ejaculatory fluid into his partner's vagina or rectum. One factor that determines the risk of transmission is the number of pinpoint breaks in the lining of the vagina or rectum. The more breaks and the more fluid coming into contact with those breaks, the greater the chance of HIV transmission.

The vagina's natural lubrication helps prevent pinpoint breaks during intercourse. Teenage girls, however, produce less vaginal fluid than adult women do. So teens are more likely to get pinpoint breaks in the vagina during intercourse and are more likely to contract HIV during unprotected sex (sex without a condom). The rectum, unlike the vagina, does not produce any natural lubrication. Therefore, more pinpoint breaks—and more instances of HIV transmission—are likely to occur during anal intercourse than during vaginal intercourse, even if the partners use an artificial lubricant.

While vaginal and anal intercourse are risky primarily for the person receiving the penis, there are also risks for the person who inserts his penis. A man may have pinpoint breaks on the skin of his penis due to injury or an infection (such as herpes or chlamydia). These pinpoint breaks can also give HIV-infected blood or vaginal fluid access to the bloodstream. Some doctors think that the virus can also enter the penis through the hole at the end.

HIV can also be transmitted through oral sex, which involves using the mouth to stimulate the penis or vagina. Oral sex is generally not as risky as vaginal or anal sex. It isn't entirely safe, however. Pinpoint breaks might exist in the skin of a person's mouth, perhaps due to a recent brushing, flossing, or gum disease. Should HIV-infected blood, semen, or vaginal secretions come in contact with one of these pinpoint breaks, HIV could enter the bloodstream through the mouth.

What Is Safer Sex?

Not having sex is the best way to avoid HIV infection. Kissing and touching do not carry a risk of HIV transmission, and these are considered safe sexual activities. But if you engage in high-risk sexual activities, such as anal or vaginal intercourse, you can help protect yourself from HIV by using a condom.

A condom is a sheath that prevents fluids from passing from or into a man's penis. AIDS professionals recommend using only latex condoms, with a water-based lubricant (available at drug stores), every time you have sexual intercourse. Condoms made of natural materials, such as lamb skin, will not protect you from HIV. Condoms are not 100 percent fail-safe. But if a man uses a condom correctly every time he has sex, his chances of either getting or transmitting HIV are minimal.

AIDS professionals also recommend using a latex barrier during oral sex. This could be a condom to cover a man's penis or a flat piece of plastic wrap, often called a "dental dam," to protect the mouth during oral sex with a woman.

If this discussion has made you uncomfortable, you are probably not alone. If you find it hard to talk and read about HIV transmission, maybe you should wait until you are older to become sexually active. Wait until a time when sexual behavior will enhance rather than complicate your life—through unplanned pregnancy or a sexually transmitted disease such as AIDS.

Even if you are not ready to have a sexual relationship, you are not too young to learn the facts about AIDS prevention. Basketball star Earvin "Magic" Johnson, diagnosed with HIV in 1991, offers the following advice to young people:

> If you decide to put off having sex, that's great. If you decide to have sex, make a conscious decision to be responsible about it. If you don't know what you're doing about sex...don't do it. Wait.

Using Condoms to Prevent HIV Infection

Latex condoms can greatly reduce a person's risk of acquiring or transmitting HIV. For condoms to provide maximum protection, they must be used from start to finish every time you have sex. Observe the following rules about correct condom use:

- ✗ Always put a condom on before intercourse.
- ✗ Open the package carefully.
- ✗ Squeeze the tip of the condom to remove any air and place the condom over the end of the erect (hard) penis.
- ✗ Continue to hold the tip of the condom and unroll it the entire length.
- ✗ Extra water-based lubrication should be used to reduce breakage. Never use an oil-based lubricant such as petroleum jelly or hand lotion, as these substances can cause condoms to break.
- ✗ Entry should be done slowly. Careless penetration can tear a condom.
- ✗ Check the condom during sex to see that it is not broken.
- ✗ If the condom should break, withdraw the penis immediately and put on a new condom.
- ✗ After ejaculation, hold onto the bottom ring of the condom and withdraw the penis while it is still erect.
- ✗ Remove and throw away the condom.

Transmission through Injecting Drug Use

Drug use is not just illegal, it can also be deadly. Drugs such as heroin, steroids, and cocaine can be injected into a vein, under the skin, or into a muscle. Many people who inject drugs share needles with other users, and HIV-infected blood is easily passed through the needle from one person's bloodstream to another's.

The best way to protect yourself from needle-based HIV transmission is to stay away from drugs. This is not always easy to do, especially for people who are addicted to drugs. If you do inject drugs, always use a new or clean needle. The Centers for Disease Control and the National Institute on Drug Abuse recommend sterilizing used hypodermic needles with bleach—although this procedure does not offer fail-safe protection against HIV.

Some cities have programs that provide clean hypodermic needles to drug users, although, as we shall learn, these programs are controversial. Most communities have treatment programs that help drug users learn to live without drugs—by far the best way to avoid needle-based HIV transmission.

Other Types of Transmission

Most HIV transmission occurs during drug use and unprotected sex. But some people have contracted HIV in different ways. An HIV-infected mother can transmit the virus to her child. During pregnancy and delivery, mother and baby can share blood. About 10 to 25 percent of babies born to mothers with HIV are infected themselves. A baby might also get HIV from an infected mother through breast milk.

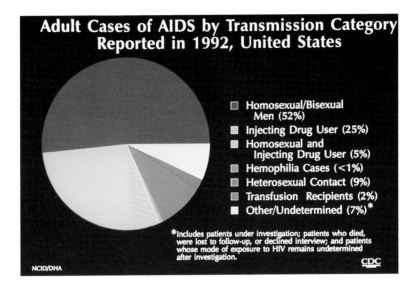

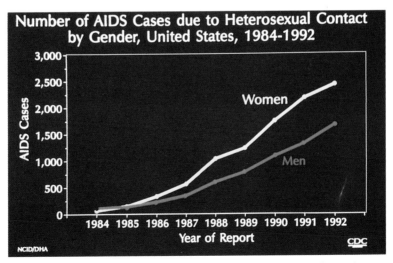

Sometimes incorrectly thought of as a "gay disease," AIDS can be spread through heterosexual contact (sex between a man and a woman). Heterosexual transmission is on the rise.

Before 1985, some people became infected with HIV through blood transfusions. Arthur Ashe, for instance, a former tennis champion, received HIV-infected blood during open-heart surgery. Ashe died of AIDS in 1993.

Elizabeth Glaser, who lost her daughter to AIDS and is herself HIV positive, speaks at the 1992 Democratic National Convention.

After the HIV test was developed, medical experts began testing blood used for transfusions and other medical procedures. The blood supply in the United States is now very safe; all donated blood products are tested for HIV. But many people who received HIV through transfusions unknowingly passed the virus on to others, often through sex.

Obstacles to Prevention

Many things can keep people from learning about AIDS prevention. One major roadblock is homophobia. Homophobia literally means fear (phobia) of homosexuals. More generally, it refers to any biases or prejudices against gay people. Many heterosexual people still think of AIDS as a "gay disease." AIDS activist Elizabeth Glaser comments:

> Because the first wave of deaths in the AIDS epidemic were gays and drug users, people were able to distance themselves and say, "[It] can't happen to me, why should I care?" AIDS also clicked into a homophobic side of America which felt that these people somehow deserved whatever happened to them. AIDS was the price you paid for an "immoral" life-style.

Many straight (heterosexual) people practice unprotected sex because they think that messages about AIDS prevention don't apply to them. But neither HIV nor AIDS discriminates. Anyone can get AIDS—gay or straight.

Another roadblock to HIV prevention is denial. HIV and AIDS make people think about death—a difficult topic for all of us. No one wants to die, but it is important to remember that death is part of the natural cycle of life. Denying this cycle can be dangerous. Healthy young people often feel that they're invulnerable to disease and death—and they often ignore warnings about safer sex. "Many youth take about as much notice of HIV infection as they do the warnings on cigarette packs," says educator Lorraine Teel.

Joel Schleusner was infected with HIV during his first sexual relationship, at age 17. "Too many young people think AIDS is an older person's illness," Joel comments. "I think way too many [young] people are avoiding safer sex."

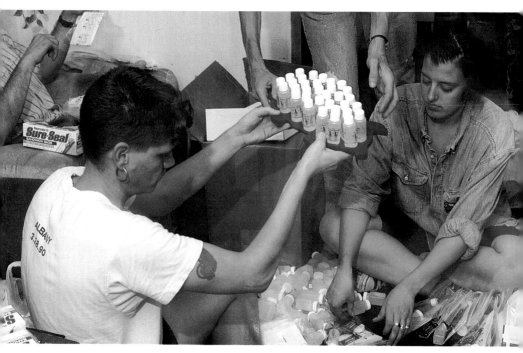

AIDS activists prepare needle-cleaning kits for distribution to drug users.

Drugs, including alcohol, can also put you at risk for HIV. Quite simply, drugs impair your judgment. If you are drunk or high, you might make a bad decision, such as choosing to have unprotected sex or using a dirty hypodermic needle. Sometimes even the rush of falling in love can impair your judgment, causing you to make unwise choices about sex. But the AIDS virus doesn't care if you are in love, drunk, or high—it just needs access to a warm, living body.

Don't let homophobia, drug use, or any other roadblocks prevent you from observing the basic rules for avoiding HIV infection:

- Learn the facts about HIV before you have sex. If you do have sex, correctly use a condom every time.
- Stay away from drugs, especially injected drugs. If you do inject drugs, use a new needle every time.

These rules will help protect you from HIV infection. Sexual and drug-using behaviors can be difficult to change. You might find it easier to change your behavior if you realize that you can get AIDS from drug use or unprotected sex. AIDS can be a killer—but one you can avoid.

THE HIV ANTIBODY TEST 4

The HIV antibody test is a blood test that determines whether or not a person has been infected with the human immunodeficiency virus. Many people mistakenly call the HIV test the "AIDS test." But the test doesn't determine whether or not you have AIDS. The test will tell you if HIV is present in your blood. People who have HIV in their blood are said to be HIV positive.

During the HIV antibody test, a vial of blood is drawn from a person's arm. The blood then undergoes either one or two tests in the laboratory. The first test is the ELISA, or the enzyme-linked immunosorbent assay. If the ELISA comes back negative, the person does not have HIV.

The ELISA has a small margin of error, however. Once in a while, the test will give a "false positive." That is, it will incorrectly say that a person has HIV. If someone's ELISA comes back positive, that person may or may not have HIV. That's why a second test is used. After a positive test result with the ELISA, the person's blood will be double-checked through another test called the Western blot. The Western blot is very reliable. If this test comes back positive, the person has HIV.

The HIV test works by determining whether antibodies to HIV are present in someone's blood. Antibodies are proteins that normally fight off viruses and other disease-causing agents. The immune system sends out antibodies when a virus attacks, much like the governor sends out the National Guard during an emergency. If the National Guard is in your town, you know there's an emergency. Likewise, if you have HIV antibodies in your blood, you know you are HIV positive. Although antibodies can destroy or disable many viruses, they can't destroy HIV.

In the United States, all blood products are tested for HIV.

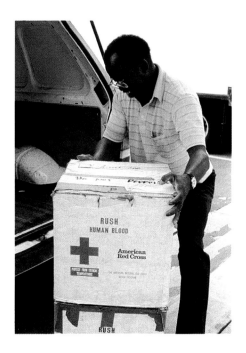

It can take up to six months after HIV transmission before the immune system produces enough antibodies to trigger the HIV test positive. This six-month delay is called the "window period." During the six-month window period, a person who is HIV positive can be tested and found to be negative. The person isn't producing enough HIV antibodies to trigger the test positive, though he or she soon will be.

Because of the window period, health-care professionals and AIDS counselors recommend that people who think they may have contracted HIV within the previous six months do one of two things: 1) wait until the window period passes and then get tested, or 2) get tested, wait for six months, and then get tested again. Of course, in between tests, people should not do anything that would allow them to get or transmit HIV—such as inject drugs or have unprotected sex.

Positive or Negative?

When the HIV test first became available to the public in the mid-1980s, some people were relieved that they could learn their HIV status. Many others were nervous about the test, fearing a positive result.

Finding out that you are HIV positive can be a frightening, disturbing, and highly emotional experience. One of the first questions people ask after a positive test result is: "How long do I have to live?" A reporter for *10 Percent* magazine interviewed young people who tested HIV positive. Here are some of their reactions:

> I didn't believe it at first. I thought HIV was something that older people got, people who had a lot of sex partners. That wasn't me. I was just getting started.

Immediately I thought I was going to die. I felt dirty and infected and bad, the way a lot of young gay men with HIV tell me they feel, because that's what society tells them.

At first I thought it was unfair and I had a lot of anger. There was a period where I just wanted to sleep, not to die, just sleep. It was so painful.

The first thing that came into my mind when I got my results was death. It was tough going to school with all these young people who were looking forward to sixty more years of life when I was thinking that I might only have ten.

Basketball player Magic Johnson speaks with young people about HIV and AIDS.

No one wants to learn that he or she has HIV. But it is important to remember that people can live for many years with HIV before they ever get sick with AIDS. Meanwhile, medical experts are working hard to develop treatments that will prolong and improve the lives of HIV-infected people.

Should You Be Tested?

If you are worried about your HIV status—for instance, if you have had unprotected sex or have injected drugs—talk to someone you trust, such as a parent, doctor, teacher, school counselor, or school nurse. You can also call a local AIDS service organization, your state AIDS information line, your state or local health department, or the CDC National AIDS Hotline at 1-800-342-AIDS. Spanish-speaking people can call La Linea Nacional de SIDA at 1-800-344-SIDA. The deaf or hearing-impaired can call 1-800-AIDS-TTY. The CDC hotline operator will explain the HIV testing process and direct you to a test site in your area. Most public test sites are free or charge only a small fee.

AIDS professionals highly recommend pre- and post-test counseling. A counselor can help determine your risks for HIV and help you deal with your fears and emotions should your test result come back positive. Sometimes a person who thinks he or she is at risk for HIV is not emotionally prepared for a positive result. A counselor might suggest to that person that he or she put off taking the HIV test. But those who put off testing should not do anything in the meantime that might expose them to HIV or allow them to pass the virus to someone else.

Protect Your Privacy

Most AIDS professionals recommend that you go to an HIV test site where your test results will be kept private and not become a matter of public record. At most test sites, you will be identified only by a number or an alias (a made-up name) rather than your real name. Under this kind of system, your HIV status cannot be revealed to anyone except you.

Although your HIV status is a private matter, you are not the only person who has a stake in knowing your test results. Your past and present sexual partners have a right to know whether or not you are HIV positive. If you are HIV positive, your sexual partners should also consider being tested for HIV. But be cautious about revealing your test results to other people—even your close friends. The HIV test has been an important tool in our fight against AIDS. But it has also opened the door for discrimination against HIV-positive people.

A COUNTRY REACTS

American society has responded to the AIDS epidemic in many different ways. Some Americans responded with fear and prejudice. But most people went to work to fight the AIDS crisis. Educators and public health professionals developed programs to teach people about AIDS prevention. Doctors developed the HIV antibody test and began searching for a cure and a vaccine. Activist groups pushed the government to spend more money on AIDS research. Many people with HIV promoted AIDS awareness and spoke out publicly against discrimination.

Although the U.S. government was at first slow to respond to the crisis, the federal government now spends billions of dollars each year to fight AIDS. The CDC was the first government agency to confront the epidemic. Other federal agencies soon followed. The National Institutes of Health (NIH) became involved in medical research, and the Food and Drug Administration (FDA) took charge of testing new AIDS drugs and safeguarding the nation's blood supply. According to the Public Health Service, the federal government budgeted approximately $6.4 billion in 1994 for HIV and

A memorial service for Americans lost to AIDS, early 1990s

AIDS research, treatment, prevention, education, and drug and vaccine development and testing.

Like the federal government, state governments help fund AIDS care, treatment, and educational programs. More and more, state boards of education are requiring AIDS education in the public schools. Some state legislatures have passed laws prohibiting discrimination against people with AIDS. Many city and county agencies provide health care and social services to people living with HIV and AIDS.

Education and Action

Not surprisingly, some of the most important work on AIDS has come from those most directly affected by the disease. The first people to organize against AIDS were gay men—many of them HIV positive. Early on in the crisis, gay men in cities across the United States formed grassroots organizations to "help their own." The money to conduct research and to care for AIDS patients came very slowly during the first few years of the epidemic. Early AIDS service organizations set out to help people with HIV, raise funds, and bring AIDS into the public eye.

These organizations have grown and most major cities now have well-established AIDS service organizations. Such groups take a fairly conservative approach to AIDS education and service. They work within the law and work closely with government agencies. But as the AIDS crisis has worn on, some people have become angry with the established political system and have taken a more radical approach to fighting AIDS. Frustrated by thousands of AIDS deaths, the lag in AIDS research, and discrimination against people with HIV, gay men in

New York City formed an organization called the AIDS Coalition to Unleash Power, or ACT UP, in the late 1980s. The group's methods include protest demonstrations and rallies.

ACT UP has pushed the government to provide more funding for research on AIDS and to make experimental AIDS drugs available more quickly. One ACT UP group

The ACT UP slogan "Silence Equals Death" reminds us that if we don't speak out in the fight against AIDS, more people will die of the disease.

Volunteers prepare the AIDS Quilt, with its thousands and thousands of panels, for display.

started an informal needle-exchange program for drug users in New York City, arranging to exchange dirty hypodermic needles for clean ones. Other ACT UP members chained themselves to the White House fence. They hoped that this protest would force the federal government to take notice and respond more quickly to the epidemic.

Another response to the AIDS epidemic does not have a political message but rather a personal one. This is the Names Project, more commonly known as the AIDS Memorial Quilt. Cleve Jones, an AIDS activist from San Francisco, got the idea for the quilt during an AIDS awareness march in the early 1980s. Jones asked demonstrators to carry signs with the names of people they knew who had died of AIDS. At the end of the march, everyone taped the hundreds of signs to the side of a building. The wall looked like a patchwork quilt. So Jones decided to create a real quilt to honor those who had died of AIDS.

Each panel of the AIDS Quilt measures six feet by three feet—the size of a human grave. Panels are made by friends, lovers, sisters, brothers, partners, and parents, and each is a personal and loving memorial to someone who died of AIDS. In addition to bearing the person's name, panels often include personal items and decorations like love letters, clothing, sequins, pearls, silk flowers, and wedding rings.

As of June 1994, the AIDS Quilt had 27,247 panels from 29 countries. It covered an area bigger than 11 football fields and weighed 32 tons. More than five million people have visited the quilt, which has been displayed around the world.

Fierce Debates

While most people agree that AIDS education is important, many parents, teachers, and community leaders do not agree on what this education should involve. Some groups feel that telling teenagers about protected sex will simply encourage them to have sex. Rather than learn about safer sex, many people argue, teenagers should be taught to abstain from sex until marriage.

Other educators feel that even if young people are taught to abstain, many will have sex anyway. If educators teach only abstinence and give no detailed information about HIV and AIDS, those young people who do have sex won't receive information that could save their lives.

We know that condom use is one way of greatly reducing the risk of HIV transmission. But some people feel that recommending condoms to teenagers will only encourage sexual activity. Former surgeon general Dr. C. Everett Koop, a leader in AIDS education, has supported teaching young people about condoms. But he has also acknowledged the complexity of the debate. In a 1987 address to members of the American Medical Association, he said:

> Some of you find it unpleasant to recommend condoms to young people. So do I. Acquired Immunodeficiency Syndrome is an unpleasant disease and recommending condoms to those who need protection is preferable to treating AIDS.

In late 1993, the federal government took a stronger stand on AIDS education by airing a series of television and radio spots about HIV. These ads were targetted at young adults and recommended condom use during sex.

Members of the Guardian Angels, an anticrime group, think that giving clean needles to drug users will only promote illegal drug use.

Another debate that has captured the nation's attention involves HIV prevention and drug use. Does distributing clean hypodermic needles to drug users simply encourage drug addiction? Many people argue that it does. Others, like members of ACT UP, believe that we should give clean needles to injecting drug users—even though drug use is illegal. ACT UP and other groups think that distributing clean needles—just like distributing condoms—is preferable to the alternative, which is letting people become infected with HIV and die of AIDS.

New Rules for a Deadly Disease

The debates over sex education, condoms, and needle exchanges are just a few of the many controversies that have surfaced during the AIDS crisis. American society has struggled with questions about AIDS in its hospitals, courtrooms, military bases—even at athletic events.

Although sex and injecting drug use are the most common methods of HIV transmission, some people have contracted HIV through contact with infected blood. The fear of this type of transmission has caused many people to call for new laws and regulations to protect the public from HIV.

For example, football players, basketball players, boxers, and other athletes often bleed during competition. What if a player were HIV positive and his or her blood came in contact with a sore or break on another player's skin? A few basketball players had just this fear after Magic Johnson announced in 1991 that he was HIV positive.

Although the risk of transmission on the playing field is extremely small, sports organizations have considered testing athletes for HIV. Most have decided against it, however, concerned that testing would violate the privacy rights of players. But in 1992, both the National Basketball Association and the National Collegiate Athletic Association instituted rules that require athletes who are bleeding to leave the court or playing field and to have their wounds bandaged.

Some people are thought to have contracted HIV in hospitals and doctors' offices—although this too is rare. Kimberly Bergalis believed she contracted HIV from her dentist during a dental procedure. Before she died in

1991, 23-year-old Bergalis spoke to Congress in support of legislation that would have required doctors and dentists to be tested for HIV and to disclose their HIV status to patients. Although the bill was defeated, several states now have laws that require health-care workers to tell their patients if they are HIV positive or have AIDS.

What about patients who are HIV positive? Should they have to reveal their HIV status to health-care workers? A small number of health-care professionals have contracted HIV, sometimes through accidental needle sticks, while treating HIV-positive patients. The law guarantees a person with HIV or AIDS the right to receive emergency medical care. But some doctors, nurses, and medical technicians have refused to treat HIV-positive or AIDS patients.

Although close to death with AIDS, Kimberly Bergalis accompanied her father to Washington, D.C., to speak in favor of mandatory HIV testing for health-care workers.

Parents and school officials wanted to keep Ryan White from attending school because he had AIDS.

People in the military, foreign service personnel, immigrants, and prisoners are required by law to take the HIV test. Some politicians have argued that government testing for HIV should be even more widespread—to include, for instance, couples who apply for marriage licenses, pregnant women, and government job applicants. Widespread testing would allow public health officials to better track the AIDS epidemic and better prevent its spread.

Most health experts agree that mandatory (required) HIV testing would be very expensive. To track the virus effectively, the government would have to test people every six months. But the strongest argument against mandatory testing is that it would violate people's rights and lead to discrimination. Test results might not be kept private, and people who were suspected of carrying HIV, such as gay men, drug users, or prostitutes, might be singled out for testing. In Cuba people with HIV are quarantined, or isolated, in government-run camps. Many Americans fear that mandatory testing would lead to similar measures in the United States.

A Fearful Society

A federal law makes it illegal to discriminate against people with AIDS or other disabilities. Technically, people cannot be fired from their jobs or made to leave school because of their HIV-positive status. Yet many people with HIV and AIDS have been victims of this type of discrimination. Some people with AIDS have been evicted from their homes. Others have been denied health insurance after testing positive for HIV.

Why are people with HIV and AIDS frequently targets of discrimination? One reason is fear. We live in a time when many illnesses can be cured. We are naturally afraid of AIDS—a disease that is almost always fatal. This fear can make us act irrationally. Even though we know that touching and hugging can't transmit HIV, we might be afraid to touch someone with AIDS. We might not want to sit near a classmate with HIV. We might ask "what if" questions: What if my lab partner has AIDS? What if I sleep on a bed on which a person with AIDS has just slept? What if I sit next to someone on the bus who is infected with HIV? Will I get HIV too?

One case that dramatically illustrates the fear of AIDS is that of Ryan White of Kokomo, Indiana. He was a teenage hemophiliac who contracted AIDS through a blood transfusion. In 1985 Kokomo officials banned 13-year-old Ryan from school, claiming his medical condition posed a health threat to other students. Hostile Kokomo residents held protests against Ryan. Local restaurants threw away plates and silverware after he had used them. Someone even shot a bullet through the Whites' living room window. Before Ryan's death in 1990, he and his family moved from Kokomo to a more tolerant community in nearby Cicero, Indiana.

Like Ryan White, Richard, Robert, and Randy Ray were banned from attending public school in Arcadia, Florida, when they were found to have HIV. The Ray brothers were all hemophiliacs who had contracted HIV from blood transfusions. In a court battle, the Rays won the right to return to public school. But the family decided to leave Arcadia after their home was destroyed by a firebomb.

Racism also plays a role in discrimination toward people with AIDS. AIDS has hit hardest in America's inner cities—where many people are poor and cut off from good medical care and from education about HIV. Drug use is more common among the poor, as is prostitution. The inner city is home to many people of color and many people with AIDS. According to the Centers for Disease Control, nearly half of those who suffer from AIDS are African American or Hispanic. Most AIDS babies are racial minorities.

Because AIDS has affected racial minorities, gay men, drug users, prostitutes, and other people on the outside of society's mainstream, middle-class Americans have been tempted to ignore the disease. Some Americans don't want their tax money spent to research AIDS or to teach students about AIDS prevention. Others don't want housing for AIDS patients located in their neighborhoods. Still others believe AIDS is a fit "punishment" for people who engage in homosexual activity or use drugs. As long as Americans think of AIDS as just a gay-person's disease, or one that affects only "bad people," not only will discrimination continue, but HIV and AIDS will keep spreading as well.

AIDS Touches All of Us

Elizabeth Glaser, the wife of actor Paul Michael Glaser, contracted the AIDS virus from a blood transfusion during childbirth. Unknowingly, she passed the virus on to

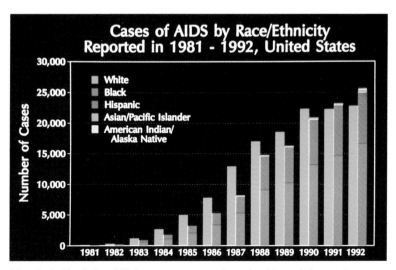

Nearly half of the AIDS cases reported in the United States have occurred in black and Hispanic people, although these groups represent only about 20 percent of the American population.

Tennis great Arthur Ashe reveals that he has AIDS at a 1992 press conference.

her two children—Jake, while he was in the womb, and Ariel, through breast-feeding. When four-year-old Ariel developed AIDS, friends were afraid to play with her and she was asked to leave school. Ariel Glaser died at age seven in 1988.

After her daughter's death, Elizabeth Glaser went on to cofound the Pediatric AIDS Foundation to assist children with HIV and AIDS. She also spoke to the nation about AIDS at the Democratic National Convention in 1992. Glaser is one of many prominent Americans who have come forward to reveal their HIV status and to fight the myths and prejudices surrounding HIV and AIDS.

Basketball great Magic Johnson has also been instrumental in increasing awareness about AIDS and in helping to educate young people. After revealing his HIV-positive status, he started the Magic Johnson Foundation to support AIDS education and prevention, to fund research, and to help care for people with AIDS.

HIV needs only a warm body to thrive. Being rich, famous, or athletic can't protect you from the virus. Rock Hudson died from AIDS in 1985. Since then, many other well-known people have been lost to the disease. Here is a list of some famous people who have died of AIDS:

Arthur Ashe, tennis player
Amanda Blake, Miss Kitty on TV's *Gunsmoke*
Tina Chow, fashion model and jewelry designer
John Curry, figure skater
Perry Ellis, fashion designer
Alison Gertz, AIDS activist
Roy Halston, fashion designer
Arturo Islas, writer
Liberace, entertainer and pianist
Stewart McKinney, U.S. congressman (R-Connecticut)
Freddie Mercury, singer and lyricist for the rock
    band Queen
Anthony Perkins, Norman Bates in Hitchcock's *Psycho*
Robert Reed, the father on *The Brady Bunch*
Max Robinson, ABC news anchor
Jerry Smith, Washington Redskin
Tom Waddell, Olympic decathlete
Ricky Wilson, guitar player for the B-52s

You probably recognize several names on this list. Maybe you even know someone who has HIV or has died from AIDS. Unfortunately, the list of famous and ordinary people with AIDS is bound to grow longer. In the final chapter, we'll take a look at what to expect from the AIDS crisis in the future.

The Future Epidemic

6

Many people now call the AIDS crisis the AIDS pandemic, which means that the epidemic has spread throughout the world. The Global AIDS Policy Coalition notes that as of January 1, 1994, more than 19 million people worldwide were thought to be infected with HIV. According to the World Health Organization (WHO), more than 980,000 AIDS cases had been reported by June 1994. But due to underreporting, WHO estimates that about 4 million AIDS cases have actually occurred to date.

Alarming Trends

The Global AIDS Policy Coalition projects that by the year 2000, 38 to 110 million adults will be infected with HIV. Poor and underdeveloped nations, particularly African nations, are expected to be hit hardest. Poor countries often can't afford to test blood supplies for HIV. Hospitals and clinics can't always afford clean hypodermic needles for medical procedures and might reuse dirty ones. Access to condoms in poor nations is limited. WHO reported in February 1992 that more than

Asian-American demonstrators in New York note that AIDS strikes people of all nationalities.

half of all people who have AIDS are Africans. About half of those are heterosexual women.

As of June 1993, more than one million babies were infected with HIV worldwide. The majority of these babies were born to women who injected drugs or had sex with an injecting drug user. The number of injecting drug

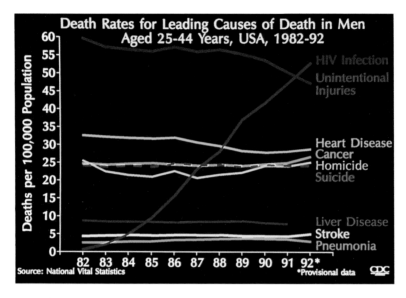

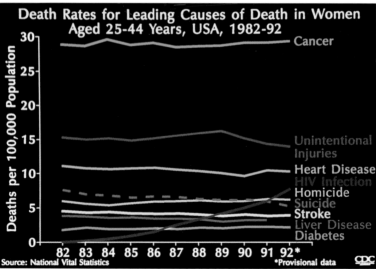

AIDS is on the rise as a major cause of death among both men and women in the United States.

users becoming infected with HIV is increasing, especially in areas where there are no needle exchanges to provide clean needles.

In the United States, 361,164 AIDS cases had been reported to the CDC by January 1994. But this number only reflects reported AIDS cases; it does not show the number of HIV-infected Americans, many of whom do not know that they have the virus. Health experts estimate that more than one million Americans are HIV positive. AIDS is the number one cause of death among American men aged 25 to 44 and the fourth leading cause of death among women aged 25 to 44. AIDS is the sixth leading cause of death among Americans aged 15 to 24.

Worldwide and in the United States, the two groups showing the greatest increase in HIV infection are women and teenagers. AIDS has moved through society in waves. Gay men were hit by the first wave of HIV infection. Hemophiliacs and drug users were in the next wave. Members of these groups passed the virus on to new groups of people, such as heterosexual women, who are part of the third wave. According to Dr. M. H. Merson, director of the WHO Global Program on AIDS, 5 of every 11 new HIV-infected people are women.

Teenagers are also part of this third wave. Dr. Merson stated at a recent AIDS conference in Berlin, Germany, that worldwide the age of HIV infection is dropping. This is partly because young people are having sex earlier—the average age of a first sexual encounter is now 15 to 16. Of AIDS cases reported in the United States, more than 14,000 have occurred in people between 13 and 24 years old.

Any Good News?

It is hard not to feel frightened and discouraged by the AIDS epidemic. There is hope, though, shown by the thousands of people who are living healthy lives, even

The red ribbons worn by these women are symbols of the fight against AIDS.

though they are carrying HIV. There is hope shown as well by the many thousands of professionals who are working full-time to stop the spread of HIV and AIDS. And while we may not yet have a vaccine or cure for AIDS, we do know how to prevent infection.

One positive example of the power of education and prevention can be seen in the gay community in the United States. The HIV infection rate among gay men has slowed significantly in the last ten years. Many gay men have become educated about HIV and now take steps to avoid the virus, such as always using a condom during sex. This effort has paid off, saving lives and decreasing the numbers of new HIV infections.

The AIDS epidemic can make the world seem like a scary place. Many people wish it were less scary, even risk-free. But the world has never been a totally safe place. We take a risk when we drive or ride in a car, and we take a risk when we have sex. No school, government, or doctor can completely remove the risk of HIV infection.

AIDS and HIV will be with us for many years. But you can reduce this risk for yourself by learning about HIV and making smart decisions. The good news is that with this book, you have the information you need to make sure that you don't become infected with HIV.

Glossary

AIDS: acquired immunodeficiency syndrome; a disease caused by the human immunodeficiency virus and characterized by the deterioration of the immune system. As the immune system breaks down, a person with AIDS becomes vulnerable to life-threatening infections and illnesses.

antibodies: proteins produced by the immune system as a defense against invading agents

blood transfusion: an injection of whole blood or plasma. Blood used for transfusions is typically donated by one person, stored in a blood bank, and injected into another person.

condom: a sheath that prevents fluid from passing into or from the penis during sexual activity

epidemic: a rapid outbreak of a disease

gay: homosexual; primarily attracted to people of the same sex

hemophilia: a blood defect that is treated with regular blood transfusions

heterosexual: primarily attracted to people of the opposite sex

HIV: human immunodeficiency virus; the virus that attacks the human immune system and causes AIDS

HIV positive: used to describe people with HIV in their bloodstreams

homophobia: the fear or hatred of homosexuals

homosexual: primarily attracted to people of the same sex

hypodermic needle: An apparatus used to inject drugs into a vein or muscle or beneath the skin

immune deficiency: a weakening of the immune system

immune system: the network of cells in the body that normally fight off disease

opportunistic infections: illnesses that commonly attack people whose immune systems have been weakened by HIV

pandemic: an epidemic occurring over a wide area and affecting a large portion of the population

safer sex: condom use to prevent HIV transmission during sex; abstaining from sexual activities that carry a risk of HIV transmission

semen: fluid secreted from the male reproductive organs during sex

T-helper cells: cells that normally warn the immune system that a virus has entered the body. HIV destroys T-helper cells.

vaccine: a preparation that enables the immune system to build resistance to a virus. Vaccines are usually derived from a weakened or killed version of the virus.

vaginal secretions: lubricants produced by the vagina during sex

virus: a disease-causing agent that can invade and reproduce inside living cells

Resources

For more information on HIV and AIDS or to find a test site in your area call directory assistance and ask for the number of your state AIDS information line. You may also call one of the following national organizations (numbers that begin with 1-800 are toll-free):

Centers for Disease Control
    CDC National AIDS Hotline: 1-800-342-AIDS
    (Spanish language): 1-800-344-SIDA
    (hearing impaired): 1-800-AIDS-TTY
    CDC National AIDS Clearinghouse: 1-800-458-5231

Other organizations
    Magic Johnson Foundation: 310-785-0201
    National Minority AIDS Council: 1-800-669-5052
    National Native American AIDS Prevention Center:
        1-800-283-AIDS
    National Sexually Transmitted Disease Hotline:
        1-800-227-8922
    National Youth Crisis Hotline: 1-800-448-4663
    Pediatric AIDS Foundation: 310-395-9051

In Canada
    Canadian AIDS Society: 613-230-3580
    Canadian Public Health Association: 613-725-3769

For information on drug addiction and treatment:
    National Institute on Drug Abuse: 1-800-662-HELP

Demonstrators hold signs bearing the names and ages of young people killed by AIDS.

Index

acquired immunodeficiency syndrome (AIDS): education about, 46–50, 65, prevention of, 9, 29–30, 32, 37, 50, 51, 65; research on, 11, 12–13, 17, 24–25; treatments for, 23–24, 25. *See also* AIDS epidemic; human immunodeficiency virus
Africa and AIDS crisis, 17, 60, 61
AIDS Coalition to Unleash Power (ACT UP), 47, 48, 51
AIDS epidemic: history of, 10–17; statistics on, 60–63
AIDS illnesses, 6, 21, 22–23. *See also* opportunistic infections
AIDS Memorial Quilt. *See* Names Project
AIDS-related dementia, 22, 23
AIDS service organizations, 12, 46
anal intercourse, 28, 29
antibodies, 39, 40
Ashe, Arthur, 34
azidothymidine (AZT), 23

babies with HIV, 14–15, 21, 32, 56, 61
Bergalis, Kimberly, 52–53
blood supplies and HIV, 14, 35, 60. *See also* HIV antibody test; HIV transmission
Buchanan, Patrick, 13

cancer and AIDS patients, 10, 22, 23
Centers for Disease Control (CDC), 10, 12, 21, 42, 44
condom use, 28, 30, 31, 37, 50, 60
Cuba and AIDS crisis, 55
cytomegalovirus (CMV), 22

discrimination against people with HIV and AIDS, 16, 46, 55–57
drug use, 8, 9, 12, 32, 37, 51, 56, 61–62. *See also* HIV transmission

enzyme-linked immunosorbent assay (ELISA), 38

Fletcher, James, 13
Food and Drug Administration, 44

Gallo, Robert, 11
Gates, Grant, 24
gay men and AIDS crisis, 8, 10, 11, 12, 13, 46, 63, 65
Gay Men's Health Crisis, 12
Glaser, Elizabeth, 35, 57–58
Global AIDS Policy Coalition, 60

health-care workers and HIV, 52–53
hemophilia, 14, 56, 63
HIV antibody test, 14, 16, 27, 35, 38–43. *See also* mandatory testing for HIV
HIV transmission: through blood transfusions, 8, 14, 34; through drug use, 8, 11, 32, 60, 62–63; through infected mother, 14, 32, 61; through sex, 8, 9, 11, 26–30, 63
homophobia, 13, 35, 57
Hudson, Rock, 15–16, 59
human immunodeficiency virus (HIV), 6, 11, 18–25; antibodies to, 39, 40; research on, 11, 12–13, 17, 24–25; vaccine for, 17, 24–25. *See also* HIV antibody test; HIV transmission

Acknowledgments

Photographs and illustrations used with permission of © Richard B. Levine: pp. 2, 45, 47, 51, 64; © Frances M. Roberts: pp. 7, 27, 36, 61, 69; Hollywood Book and Poster: p. 15; © Ed Kashi: pp. 16, 20; Dr. Didier Trono, The Salk Institute for Biological Studies: p. 19; National Cancer Institute: p. 23; Centers for Disease Control: pp. 33 (both), 57, 62 (both); Reuters/Bettman: pp. 34, 58; American Red Cross: p. 39; Magic Johnson Foundation: p. 41; Names Project/Mark Theissen: p. 48; UPI/Bettmann: pp. 53, 54; © Gabe Kirchheimer: p. 72.

Cover photograph: © Ed Kashi.

Students view the AIDS Memorial Quilt in Arcata, California.